When the egg began to **crack**,
the knight thought, **this looks bad . . .**

P9-EJZ-232

But a little **dragon's head**
popped out,
puffed **smoke**,
and **gargled** . . .

"Dad?"

Now since **Sir Kindly** had no child
he took the **dragon** home
and asked his **lady wife**
if they could raise him as their **own**.

His scales were **hard**,
his claws were **sharp**,
but **Lady Kindly** knew
that she would **love** him
as her own **however**
big he grew.

They taught young Scaly **lessons**
and the very **first** he learnt,
was that breathing fire was
not allowed
(in case someone got burnt).

They packed the little fellow
off to **Knight School** in a wagon,
with **fingers crossed** that no one
would be **beastly** to their dragon.

Three **rasty** student knights
– who l:ked being **mean** and **cruel** –
did **everything** they could to
make it hard for him at school.

They picked the nickname Scaly Pants
and tried to **bully** him.
But words, like arrows, **bounced** right off
his thick green **dragon skin**.

He **studied hard** for many years . . .

learnt how to **ride** and **fight**.

Till he graduated as
the one-and-only . . .

Dragon
Knight!

He made one very **special friend**,
and held that friendship **dear**,
the plucky little **horse** he rode,
the filly, Guinevere.

One day a ghastly **giant**
chanced upon their peaceful land.
He **stomped** through town
(knocked buildings down),
grabbed cows in either hand.

He **stuffed** his pockets full of geese,
drained barrels dry of beer,
ate anyone who crossed his path,
and burped . . .

The people cried, "Oh! Help us, please!"
and ran to beg the King,
"Your Majesty, please send a knight
to save us from this thing."

The King said, "All you knights must go.
Consider it a test.
The knight who beats the giant
I'll proclaim to be the best."

The **Nasty Knights** raced on ahead,
each on a **mighty steed**,
with Scaly trailing far behind
(at a somewhat **slower** speed).

When he arrived, the Nasty Knights were tied tight to a tree.
They stopped their blubbing and cried out, "Oh, Scaly, set us free!"
They begged him, "Don't forsake us! We've always been your friends.
Please don't leave your pals to such a ghastly, gruesome end.'

The Giant stomped towards him.
Its breath was rank and rotten.
Its red beard filled with bits of food
from dinners long forgotten.

It bent down, **belched**, and picked a pound of **bogey** from its nose.

He **flicked** it at Scaly, scoffing, "You're the **hero**, I suppose?"

He grabbed poor Scaly's bony leg
with a giant, hairy limb.

Then took a sniff . . .

and licked
his lips . . .

and promptly
swallowed him.

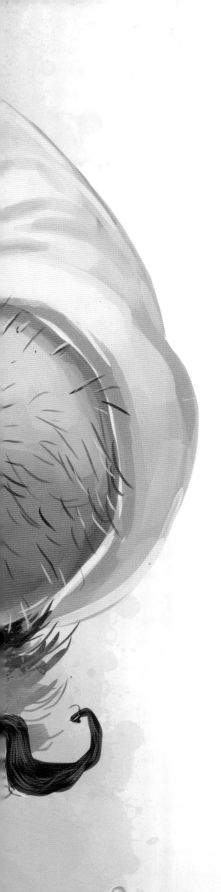

But Gwinny ran to save him,
and, between the giant's feet,
she found the sword that Scaly dropped
and grabbed it with her teeth.

She jabbed the giant in his toe.
He jumped and gave a shout . . .

. . . his **slimy** mouth gaped open **wide**
and Scaly **plopped** right out.

As Scaly fell he **grabbed** a rope
– and – what a stroke of **luck**!

It was the one that held the
giant's **stinky trousers up.**

Like a circus tent **collapsing,**
his trousers hit the **floor.**

And with a blush, he pulled
them up, and shouted,

"This means **war!**"

He **chased** them to the edge of town –
they **nearly** got away.
But when Scaly yelled,
"Go faster, Gwinn!"
she fell and panted, "Neigh!"

Scaly drew his **sword** and stood there ready to **defend**,
but the giant **swatted** him away and **grabbed** his little friend.

"I wish I'd time," the giant said,
"to **grind** her bones for bread,
but the chase has left me **peckish**
and **it's time that I was fed**."

His mouth was gaping **wide** and **dark**.
This is it! thought Gwinny.
She put her head between her hooves
and gave a little whinny.

But Scaly wasn't beaten.
There was **one last thing** to try.
He **knew** Mummy wouldn't like it,
but his best friend **couldn't** die.

He drew the **deepest breath** he could,
and **carefully** took aim.

Then **blasted** out a never-ending stream of **dragon flame.**

"Me **bum's** on **fire!**"

the giant shrieked.

His underpants were smoking.
And since he hadn't washed for months
the smell had Scaly choking!

The giant **leapt** into a lake,
which turned to **clouds** of **steam**,
then **legged** it sharpish from the Realm,
and **never more was seen**.

The news of Scaly's triumph
quickly spread throughout the land.
Till he knelt before the king
who stood with regal sword in hand.

He said, "Arise, Sir Scaly Pants. You've proved you have the right to call yourself my Champion, and the Bravest Dragon Knight."

So that is how Sir Scaly and his little horse found glory. And started their adventures ... but that's another story